Once
a
Cheater

Rachael Reed
©2024

Chapter 1: Perfect on Paper

Isis sat on the worn-out couch, her four-year-old daughter, Kiana, nestled in her lap, watching cartoons. The small apartment was cozy but cramped, a reflection of her tireless efforts to make a home despite the chaos Jamal brought into their lives. She sighed, running her fingers through Kiana's curls, trying to push away the thoughts of where Jamal might be.

The phone rang, its shrill tone cutting through the quiet. Isis grabbed it, her heart sinking as she saw the number. She answered reluctantly, already knowing what was coming.

"Hello?"

"Isis, girl, you need to know your man out here wildin' again. I saw him with some chick at the club last night."

Isis clenched her jaw, trying to keep her voice steady. "Thanks for lettin' me know, Tasha. I appreciate it."

She hung up, feeling the familiar sting of betrayal. Jamal had been her world for over ten years, but he was always for the streets. His cheating, his shady dealings, it was all part of the package she'd been carrying for too long. She glanced at Kiana, feeling a surge of determination. She had to hold it together for her daughter, no matter what.

Just then, the door creaked open, and Jamal stumbled in, smelling of booze and cheap perfume. He barely acknowledged her, heading straight for the bedroom.

"Jamal," she called after him, her voice tinged with frustration. "We need to talk."

He turned, his eyes bloodshot and unfocused. "Ain't nothin' to talk about, Isis. I'm tired."

Isis stood, placing Kiana gently on the couch. "Tired? You think I'm not tired? I'm here holdin' down the fort while you out doin' God knows what."

Jamal waved her off, slumping onto the bed. "I said I'm tired. We'll talk later."

She watched him, her anger simmering just below the surface. This was her life—constantly picking up the pieces, trying to make sense of the chaos he brought. But she was done being just the perfect girlfriend. She needed more.

The next day, Isis was at work, trying to focus on her job at the clinic, but her mind kept drifting. Jamal's neglect, his affairs, the calls from other women—it was all too much. She needed help, and the only person she could think to call was Jowan, Jamal's brother. Jowan had always been there for her, reliable and steady, the opposite of Jamal.

During her lunch break, she dialed Jowan's number.

"Hey, Jowan. It's Isis. Can you come by later? I need some help with a few things around the house."

"No problem, Isis. I'll be there after work."

That evening, Jowan showed up, his usual calm presence a balm to her frayed nerves. He fixed the leaky faucet, changed the lightbulbs, and even played with Kiana, bringing a rare smile to her face.

"You always know how to fix things, Jowan," she said, grateful.

He shrugged, a small smile playing on his lips. "Just doin' what I can. You deserve better, Isis. You know that, right?"

Isis looked away, feeling a mix of emotions. She knew he was right, but admitting it felt like a betrayal. "It's complicated, Jowan. Jamal... he's Kiana's father."

"I get that. But you gotta think about what's best for you and Kiana. You can't keep livin' like this."

His words lingered in her mind long after he left. She sat on the couch, watching Kiana sleep, her heart heavy with the weight of her choices. She loved Jamal, but love wasn't enough to keep the pain at bay. She needed to make a change, but the thought of doing it alone terrified her.

The next morning, Jamal was gone before she woke up, leaving behind the usual mess. As she cleaned up, her phone buzzed with another message from Tasha, this time with a picture of Jamal and some woman, all over each other at the club. Isis felt a surge of anger and hurt, the final straw breaking the camel's back.

She dialed Jowan's number again, her hands shaking. "Jowan, can you come by tonight? I need to talk."

"Of course, Isis. I'll be there."

That night, as Jowan sat across from her, she finally let the tears fall. "I can't do this anymore, Jowan. Jamal... he's breaking me."

Jowan reached out, taking her hand. "You don't have to do it alone, Isis. I'm here for you, whatever you need."

Isis looked into his eyes, seeing the sincerity and care she had been missing for so long. For the first time, she felt a glimmer of hope. Maybe, just maybe, she could find a way out of this darkness.

As the night wore on, they talked and shared their frustrations, the bond between them growing stronger. Jowan was everything Jamal wasn't—kind, supportive, and dependable. And as the lines blurred between friendship and something more, Isis realized she was standing on the edge of a decision that could change everything.

Chapter 2: Dependence on Jowan

Isis woke up to the sound of Kiana's laughter echoing through the small apartment. She stretched and glanced at the clock—6:30 AM. Another day, another hustle. Jamal had been MIA since the argument, and she hadn't heard a peep from him. Typical.

She got up, moving through the motions of getting Kiana ready for daycare. The little girl's bright smile was a stark contrast to the heaviness in Isis's heart. "Come on, baby. Time to get you dressed," she said, trying to muster some enthusiasm.

Once Kiana was settled, Isis grabbed her phone and dialed Jowan. She hated relying on him so much, but with Jamal out of the picture, she had no choice.

"Hey, Jowan. Can you come by after work? The sink's acting up again, and I could use some help with a few things."

Jowan's voice was steady and reassuring. "Of course, Isis. I'll be there around six."

The day dragged on, each hour blurring into the next. At the clinic, Isis struggled to keep her focus, her mind constantly drifting back to Jamal's betrayal and Jowan's steady presence. She couldn't shake the feeling that her life was teetering on the edge of something she couldn't quite grasp.

When she got home, the sight of Jamal lounging on the couch with a beer in hand nearly sent her over the edge. He looked up, a lazy grin spreading across his face. "Hey, baby. Miss me?"

Isis clenched her fists, trying to keep her cool. "Where you been, Jamal? You think you can just waltz back in here like nothin' happened?"

Jamal shrugged, taking a swig of his beer. "I'm here now, ain't I? Why you always trippin'?"

Before Isis could respond, there was a knock at the door. She opened it to find Jowan standing there, a toolbox in hand. His eyes flicked to Jamal, and his expression hardened.

"Hey, Jowan. Thanks for coming," Isis said, stepping aside to let him in.

Jamal's grin faded as he sat up. "What's he doin' here?"

Isis ignored him, focusing on Jowan. "The sink's been leaking again, and I need some help with a few other things around the house."

Jowan nodded, moving past Jamal without a word. He went straight to the kitchen, setting to work on the sink. Jamal watched him, his eyes narrowing.

"What's up with this, Isis? You callin' my brother to do my job now?"

Isis turned to him, her voice steady. "Your job? When's the last time you fixed anything around here, Jamal? You're too busy runnin' the streets to take care of your own family."

Jamal stood up, his temper flaring. "Don't talk to me like that. You know what I gotta do to survive out there."

Jowan's voice cut through the tension. "Maybe if you spent more time takin' care of your family and less time in the streets, you wouldn't have to worry about that."

Jamal's fists clenched, and he took a step toward Jowan. "You think you can come in here and play hero? This is my house."

Jowan didn't back down, meeting his brother's glare head-on. "Then act like it, Jamal. Step up and be a man."

Isis's heart pounded in her chest, the tension between the two men palpable. She stepped between them, her voice shaking. "Enough. This ain't solving anything."

Jamal glared at her, then at Jowan, before storming out of the apartment, slamming the door behind him. The sound echoed through the small space, leaving an uneasy silence in its wake.

Jowan sighed, turning back to the sink. "I'm sorry, Isis. I didn't mean to cause more trouble."

Isis shook her head, tears stinging her eyes. "It's not your fault. He's been like this for years. I just... I don't know what to do anymore."

Jowan finished fixing the sink and straightened up, his eyes filled with concern. "You deserve better than this, Isis. You and Kiana both."

Isis wiped her eyes, feeling a surge of gratitude and something deeper. "Thank you, Jowan. For everything."

He smiled softly. "I'm always here for you. You know that."

As Jowan gathered his tools and prepared to leave, Isis felt a wave of emotions crash over her. She watched him, her mind racing. She knew she was falling for him, and it terrified her. But the way he looked at her, the way he cared for her and Kiana—it was everything she'd been missing with Jamal.

Later that night, as she lay in bed, Isis couldn't stop thinking about Jowan. She knew things were changing, and she had to make some tough decisions. The life she wanted was within reach, but it meant letting go of the one she'd known for so long.

Isis took a deep breath, her resolve hardening. She would do whatever it took to build a better life for herself and her daughter. And if that meant letting go of Jamal and embracing the feelings she had for Jowan, then so be it. It was time for a change, and she was ready to fight for her happiness.

Chapter 3: Growing Closer

Isis was sittin' at the kitchen table, her head in her hands, the weight of her world pressing down on her. Jamal had been gone for three days straight, not a call, not a text. Kiana was playing with her dolls in the living room, her innocent laughter a painful reminder of the chaos that surrounded them.

Her phone buzzed. It was a text from Jowan.

Jowan: "Need any help today? I'm free after 5."

Isis's heart skipped a beat. She quickly replied.

Isis: "Yeah, can you come by? Got a few things that need fixin'. Thanks."

By the time Jowan arrived, the sun was settin', casting long shadows through the apartment. Isis opened the door, and the sight of him standing there brought a wave of relief.

"Hey, Jowan. Thanks for coming."

Jowan smiled, stepping inside. "No problem, Isis. What needs fixin' today?"

Isis gestured toward the sink. "The garbage disposal's actin' up again. And I think the light in Kiana's room is about to go out."

Jowan nodded, rolling up his sleeves. "Got it. I'll take care of it."

As he worked, Isis watched him, feelin' a mix of gratitude and somethin' deeper. He moved with confidence, his presence calming the storm that raged in her life. She realized how much she depended on him, not just for the practical things, but for the emotional support he provided.

"Jowan," she said softly, "I don't know what I'd do without you."

He looked up, his eyes meeting hers. "You don't have to do it alone, Isis. I'm always here for you."

Her heart ached with the truth of his words. She wanted to tell him how she felt, but fear held her back. Instead, she smiled and nodded, trying to keep her emotions in check.

Later, after Kiana was in bed, Jowan and Isis sat on the couch, the air between them thick with unspoken words. Jowan's arm rested on the back of the couch, close enough that Isis could feel his warmth.

"Isis, can I ask you somethin'?" Jowan said, his voice low.

"Of course," she replied, her heart beating faster.

"Why do you stay with Jamal? You deserve so much better."

Isis sighed, the question cutting deep. "I don't know. Maybe I'm scared. Scared of being alone, scared of starting over. But mostly, I stay for Kiana. She needs her father."

Jowan nodded, understanding in his eyes. "I get that. But you can't keep sacrificin' your happiness for him. You deserve to be happy, too."

Isis looked down, tears welling up in her eyes. "I know. It's just... so hard."

Jowan reached out, his hand gently lifting her chin so she could meet his gaze. "You're not alone, Isis. I'm here. And I care about you. More than you know."

The intensity of his words hit her like a tidal wave. Before she could second-guess herself, she leaned in, their lips meeting in a soft, tentative kiss. It was a moment of pure connection, a spark in the darkness.

When they pulled away, Jowan's eyes were filled with emotion. "Isis, I've wanted to tell you for so long. I'm in love with you."

Isis's breath caught in her throat. She had known it, felt it, but hearing it out loud made it real. "I love you too, Jowan. I've been so afraid to admit it, but I can't deny it anymore."

Jowan smiled, pulling her into his arms. "We'll figure this out together, Isis. You don't have to be afraid."

As they sat there, wrapped in each other's embrace, Isis felt a sense of peace she hadn't known in years. For the first time, she saw a future filled with hope and love, a future where she didn't have to carry the weight alone.

But the reality of their situation loomed large. Jamal was still out there, and the streets were unforgiving. They would have to navigate the dangers and uncertainties, but Isis knew one thing for sure: with Jowan by her side, she was ready to face whatever came their way.

The night deepened, and as they talked and planned, the bond between them grew stronger. Isis knew the road ahead would be tough, but she also knew that she had found something worth fighting for. And fight she would, with everything she had.

Chapter 4: The Affair Begins

Isis sat on her porch, the night air heavy with the scent of summer and the distant hum of the city. She couldn't shake the memory of Jowan's kiss, the warmth of his touch still lingering on her lips. It felt right, but the guilt gnawed at her. She was playing with fire, and she knew it.

Her phone buzzed, pulling her out of her thoughts. It was a text from Jowan.

Jowan: "Can I see you tonight?"

Isis hesitated, her heart racing. She knew she should say no, but the pull was too strong.

Isis: "Yeah, come by around 9. Kiana will be asleep."

She put her phone down, trying to steady her breathing. The risk was high, but she couldn't deny her feelings any longer. She needed Jowan, and he needed her.

When Jowan arrived, the air was charged with anticipation. He stepped onto the porch, his eyes meeting hers with a mix of desire and worry.

"Isis," he said softly, taking her hand. "You sure about this?"

She nodded, pulling him inside. "I'm sure, Jowan. I need you."

As soon as the door closed, their lips met in a heated kiss. The tension between them snapped, replaced by a rush of passion. They moved to the bedroom, the world outside forgotten.

Hours later, they lay tangled in the sheets, the room filled with the scent of their lovemaking. Jowan traced patterns on her skin, his touch gentle.

"This feels so right, Isis," he murmured. "But what about Jamal?"

Isis sighed, her heart heavy with conflicting emotions. "I don't know. He's out there doin' his thing, not carin' about us. I can't keep living like this, Jowan. I need to be happy."

Jowan kissed her forehead, his voice firm. "We'll figure it out. Together."

But as the days turned into weeks, their secret affair became harder to hide. The streets had eyes, and whispers started to spread. Jamal's absences grew longer, his activities more reckless. He was spiraling, and Isis knew it was only a matter of time before everything came crashing down.

One night, as Isis was getting ready for bed, her phone rang. It was one of Jamal's side chicks, her voice dripping with spite.

"Yo, Isis. Thought you should know, Jamal's been messin' with me. And he ain't comin' home tonight."

Isis's anger flared. She was done with the lies, the betrayal. She hung up, her mind made up. She texted Jowan.

Isis: "I need to see you. Now."

He arrived minutes later, concern etched on his face. "What's wrong, Isis?"

She met his eyes, her resolve hardening. "I'm done with Jamal. I can't do this anymore. I want to be with you."

Jowan pulled her into his arms, his voice soothing. "I'm here, Isis. We'll get through this."

But as they stood there, the door burst open. Jamal stumbled in, his eyes bloodshot, a wild look on his face.

"What the fuck is this?" he slurred, his gaze shifting between them.

Isis stepped forward, her voice shaking but firm. "Jamal, it's over. I can't do this anymore. You need to leave."

Jamal's anger exploded. "You think you can just throw me out? This is my house!"

Jowan moved between them, his voice calm but firm. "Jamal, you need to go. Don't make this worse."

Jamal lunged at Jowan, fists swinging. They crashed into the coffee table, the sound of breaking glass echoing through the room. Isis screamed, trying to pull them apart, but Jamal was out of control.

"Stop it! Both of you!" she cried, but they were locked in a brutal struggle.

Finally, Jowan managed to pin Jamal down, his voice deadly calm. "You need to get out, Jamal. Don't come back."

Jamal glared up at him, his face twisted with rage. "This ain't over, Jowan. I'll make you pay for this."

He stormed out, slamming the door behind him. Isis collapsed onto the couch, her body trembling. Jowan sat beside her, pulling her into his arms.

"It's gonna be okay, Isis," he whispered. "We'll get through this."

But deep down, Isis knew the worst was yet to come. Jamal wasn't the type to let things go, and the danger they faced was far from over. As she clung to Jowan, the reality of their situation hit her hard. They were in too deep, and there was no turning back.

The next morning, Isis woke up to a pounding headache and a sense of dread. She had crossed a line, and there was no going back. But for the first time in a long time, she felt a glimmer of hope. She had Jowan, and together, they would face whatever came their way.

As the sun rose over the city, casting long shadows on the streets below, Isis steeled herself for the fight ahead. She was ready to take control of her life, to build a future with the man she loved. No matter the cost, she was determined to find happiness and freedom. The battle had just begun, and she was ready to win.

Chapter 5: The Tipping Point

Isis sat on the edge of her bed, the morning light barely filtering through the curtains. The apartment felt like a ticking time bomb, every creak and groan of the building amplifying her anxiety. She hadn't slept much, the events of the previous night playing on a loop in her mind. Jamal's threat echoed in her head: "This ain't over. I'll make you pay for this."

She rubbed her temples, trying to clear the fog. Kiana was still asleep, blissfully unaware of the chaos that threatened to upend their lives. Isis knew she had to stay strong for her daughter, but the weight of it all was crushing.

Her phone buzzed on the nightstand. It was Jowan.

Jowan: "Morning. How you holdin' up?"

Isis: "Barely. Can you come over?"

Jowan: "Be there in 10."

Isis exhaled, feeling a slight relief. Jowan's presence was the only thing keeping her grounded. She got up, splashed some water on her face, and made her way to the kitchen. As she put on a pot of coffee, there was a knock at the door. She opened it to find Jowan, his expression tense but comforting.

"Hey," he said, stepping inside and pulling her into a hug. "You okay?"

She nodded against his chest, feeling his strength seep into her. "I'm tryin' to be. I just... I'm scared, Jowan. Jamal's not gonna let this go."

Jowan's jaw tightened. "We'll handle it. I won't let him hurt you or Kiana."

They sat at the kitchen table, the silence between them filled with unspoken fears. Isis sipped her coffee, her mind racing with possibilities. She knew they had to be smart, had to stay ahead of Jamal's moves.

Suddenly, there was a loud bang on the door, making Isis jump. She glanced at Jowan, her heart pounding.

"Who is it?" Jowan called out, standing protectively in front of Isis.

"It's Marcus," came the reply, the voice familiar but strained.

Jowan opened the door to reveal Marcus, one of Jamal's closest friends. His face was bruised, and he looked like he hadn't slept.

"Marcus, what the hell happened to you?" Jowan asked, pulling him inside.

Marcus slumped into a chair, wincing in pain. "Jamal's losin' it, man. He's been wildin' out since last night. He's talkin' crazy, sayin' he's gonna come after y'all."

Isis felt a chill run down her spine. "What do you mean, come after us?"

Marcus shook his head, his eyes filled with regret. "He thinks y'all been plottin' against him. He's convinced himself you and Jowan are tryin' to take him out. He's gatherin' his boys, talkin' 'bout makin' an example outta y'all."

Jowan's fists clenched. "We need to get you somewhere safe, Isis. This is gettin' outta hand."

Isis nodded, her fear morphing into determination. "What do we do?"

Jowan stood up, his mind racing. "We need to lay low for a bit, let things cool off. Marcus, you know where Jamal's at right now?"

Marcus nodded. "Yeah, he's holed up at Keisha's spot. But he's got eyes everywhere. You gotta be careful."

Isis looked at Jowan, her voice steady. "We need to get Kiana and get outta here. Now."

They moved quickly, packing essentials and grabbing Kiana, who was still groggy from sleep. Isis felt a pang of guilt seeing the confusion in her daughter's eyes, but she knew they had no choice.

As they loaded up the car, Jowan turned to Isis. "I know a place we can go. It's out of the city, safe. We'll figure out our next move from there."

Isis nodded, trusting him completely. "Let's go."

They drove through the city, every shadow and corner feeling like a threat. Isis kept glancing at the rearview mirror, half-expecting to see Jamal's car tailing them. But the streets were empty, the city oblivious to their escape.

When they finally reached the safe house, a small cabin on the outskirts, Isis felt a wave of relief. It was isolated, surrounded by trees, the perfect hideaway.

Jowan helped carry their bags inside, his eyes scanning the surroundings. "We'll be safe here. At least for now."

Isis set Kiana down on the couch, wrapping her in a blanket. She turned to Jowan, her eyes filled with gratitude. "Thank you, Jowan. For everything."

He pulled her into a hug, his voice gentle. "We'll get through this, Isis. Together."

But as they settled in, the reality of their situation loomed large. They were safe for now, but Jamal was still out there, a ticking time bomb. Isis knew they had to stay vigilant, had to be ready for whatever came next.

As the night fell, Isis and Jowan sat on the porch, the darkness surrounding them. They talked about their fears, their hopes, and their plans for the future. Isis felt a sense of peace, knowing she wasn't alone in this fight. She had Jowan by her side, and together, they were stronger than anything Jamal could throw at them.

But deep down, she knew the battle was far from over. The streets were unforgiving, and Jamal's rage was a force to be reckoned with. Isis steeled herself, ready to face whatever came their way. She had found love in the midst of chaos, and she wasn't about to let it slip away.

As the stars twinkled above, Isis made a silent promise to herself: she would protect her family, no matter the cost. The fight was just beginning, and she was ready to do whatever it took to win.

Chapter 6: Uncertainty and Discovery

The cabin's creaky floorboards echoed under Isis's feet as she paced back and forth, anxiety clawing at her insides. Outside, the night was eerily quiet, a stark contrast to the chaotic noise of the city streets she was used to. She felt like a prisoner, trapped by the decisions that had led her to this moment.

Jowan sat at the small kitchen table, his eyes following her every move. "Isis, you gotta calm down. Stressin' ain't gonna help."

She stopped and faced him, frustration etched on her face. "How am I supposed to calm down, Jowan? Jamal's out there, and he's gunnin' for us. I feel like we're sittin' ducks."

Jowan stood up and walked over to her, placing his hands on her shoulders. "We got each other, and we got a plan. We gonna get through this. Trust me."

Isis nodded, but the fear in her chest didn't ease. She glanced over at Kiana, who was playing quietly in the corner with her dolls, blissfully unaware of the danger lurking just beyond the trees.

The sound of a car approaching made her heart skip a beat. She and Jowan exchanged a tense look, both of them reaching for the guns they had stashed away for protection. The headlights pierced through the darkness, stopping just short of the cabin.

Jowan peered out the window, then relaxed slightly. "It's Marcus."

Isis exhaled a breath she hadn't realized she was holding. Marcus stepped out of the car, looking around cautiously before heading to the door. Jowan opened it, letting him in.

"Y'all good?" Marcus asked, his eyes darting around the room.

"We're fine," Jowan replied. "What's goin' on?"

Marcus sat down heavily, rubbing his face. "Jamal's been on a rampage. He's gettin' more reckless, more dangerous. Word is, he's been talkin' to some heavy hitters, tryin' to get them on his side."

Isis felt a chill run down her spine. "What do we do?"

Marcus looked at her, his expression serious. "We need to stay one step ahead. I got a guy who can help, but it's gonna cost. And we need to be smart about it."

Jowan nodded. "We got the money. Whatever it takes."

As they discussed their next steps, Isis's mind drifted to her growing belly. She hadn't told Jowan yet, but the uncertainty of the baby's paternity weighed heavily on her. She needed to know, for her own peace of mind.

After Marcus left, she sat down with Jowan, taking his hand. "There's something I need to tell you."

Jowan's eyes were filled with concern. "What is it, Isis?"

She took a deep breath, her voice trembling. "I'm pregnant. And I don't know if the baby is yours or Jamal's."

Jowan's expression softened, and he pulled her into a hug. "We'll figure it out. No matter what, I'm here for you and the baby. We're in this together."

Isis felt tears prick at her eyes. "Thank you, Jowan. I don't know what I'd do without you."

He kissed her forehead, his voice steady and reassuring. "You'll never have to find out."

The days passed in a blur of planning and preparation. They kept a low profile, relying on Marcus for updates and support. Every time a car passed by or a twig snapped in the woods, Isis's heart would race, but Jowan's presence kept her grounded.

One afternoon, while Jowan was out gathering supplies, Isis decided to take a walk around the property. She needed fresh air, a break from the constant tension. As she walked, she thought about the future, about what kind of life she wanted for herself and her children.

Her thoughts were interrupted by the sound of footsteps behind her. She turned, her hand instinctively reaching for the gun in her waistband. But it was Jowan, carrying a bag of groceries and looking concerned.

"You okay?" he asked, setting the bag down and walking over to her.

Isis nodded, trying to smile. "Just needed some air. It's hard bein' cooped up all the time."

Jowan took her hand, his touch warm and comforting. "I know. But we're almost through this. We just gotta stay strong a little longer."

Isis leaned into him, drawing strength from his presence. "I'm scared, Jowan. What if Jamal finds us?"

He held her close, his voice firm. "He won't. We're gonna protect our family. No matter what."

As the sun began to set, casting long shadows across the yard, Isis felt a flicker of hope. They had been through so much, but they were still standing. Together, they could face whatever came their way.

The night was filled with plans and whispers, a constant reminder of the battle they were fighting. But for the first time in a long time, Isis felt a sense of peace. She had Jowan, she had hope, and she had the determination to see this through.

As they settled in for the night, the cabin feeling a little more like home, Isis knew that the road ahead was still filled with danger. But she was ready to face it head-on, with Jowan by her side. The streets were ruthless, but love was stronger. And Isis was determined to protect what mattered most.

Chapter 7: Confrontation

Isis sat on the edge of the bed, her mind racing. The safe house felt suffocating, the walls closing in on her as the reality of their situation settled in. Kiana played quietly on the floor, unaware of the storm brewing outside. Isis knew they couldn't hide forever. Jamal's rage was like a ticking time bomb, and it was only a matter of time before he found them.

The sound of a car approaching made her heart skip a beat. She peeked through the curtains, relief washing over her when she saw Jowan and Marcus stepping out. She opened the door, letting them in, but the tension in their faces told her something was wrong.

"What happened?" she asked, her voice shaking.

Jowan looked grim, his eyes dark with worry. "We got a problem, Isis. Jamal's makin' moves. He's got some serious muscle backing him now. We need to be ready."

Isis felt a chill run down her spine. "What do we do?"

Marcus stepped forward, his voice low and urgent. "We need to confront him. Make him understand he ain't gonna get away with this. We hit him where it hurts."

Jowan nodded, his jaw set. "We need to take the fight to him. Show him we ain't afraid."

Isis's heart pounded in her chest. The thought of facing Jamal terrified her, but she knew they had no choice. She looked at Jowan, drawing strength from his determination. "Okay. Let's do this."

They spent the next few hours planning their move, mapping out the best way to confront Jamal and his crew. Isis felt a surge of resolve, her fear transforming into a fierce determination. She would protect her family, no matter what.

As night fell, they set out, the city's streets a maze of shadows and danger. The tension was palpable, every noise making Isis jump. They reached the old warehouse where Jamal was holed up, the place a fortress of grime and decay.

Jowan turned to Isis, his eyes filled with intensity. "Stay close. We stick to the plan."

Isis nodded, gripping the handle of the gun Marcus had given her. She felt the weight of it in her hand, a cold reminder of the violence that might come. They moved silently, slipping into the warehouse, the darkness swallowing them whole.

Inside, the air was thick with the stench of sweat and smoke. Voices echoed through the halls, angry and threatening. Jamal's crew was on high alert, but they hadn't seen them yet. Jowan signaled for them to split up, and Isis felt her pulse quicken as she followed him deeper into the labyrinth.

They found Jamal in the main room, surrounded by his cronies. He looked up, his eyes narrowing when he saw them. "Well, well, well. Look who decided to show up."

Jowan stepped forward, his voice cold and steady. "It's over, Jamal. You need to back off. Leave Isis and Kiana alone."

Jamal laughed, a harsh, mocking sound. "You think you can just waltz in here and tell me what to do? You got some nerve, Jowan."

Isis's hand tightened on the gun, her heart pounding. She stepped beside Jowan, her voice shaking but firm. "This ends now, Jamal. We ain't scared of you."

Jamal's eyes flashed with anger. "You think you can take me down? You're nothin'. Both of you."

The tension snapped like a rubber band. Jamal lunged at Jowan, fists flying. The room erupted into chaos, bodies clashing, shouts filling the air. Isis watched in horror as Jowan and Jamal fought, their rage a brutal dance of violence.

She raised the gun, her hands shaking. "Stop it! Both of you, stop!"

But they were locked in a deadly struggle, oblivious to her cries. Marcus grabbed one of Jamal's men, slamming him into the wall. The sound of gunfire echoed through the warehouse, a terrifying reminder of the stakes.

Isis took a deep breath, her resolve hardening. She aimed at the ceiling and fired, the deafening sound bringing everything to a halt. "Enough!"

Jamal froze, his eyes wild with fury. "You gonna shoot me, Isis? Go ahead. Do it."

Isis's hands trembled, but she held her ground. "This has to stop. Now."

Jowan, breathing hard, stepped back, his eyes never leaving Jamal. "You heard her. It's over."

Jamal's gaze flickered between them, his anger palpable. But something in Isis's eyes made him hesitate. He lowered his fists, a bitter smile twisting his lips. "This ain't over. You hear me? This ain't over."

He turned and stormed out, his men following reluctantly. The silence that followed was deafening, the tension hanging heavy in the air. Isis lowered the gun, her whole body shaking.

Jowan wrapped his arms around her, his voice soothing. "You did good, Isis. It's gonna be okay."

Isis clung to him, tears streaming down her face. "I'm so scared, Jowan. What if he comes back?"

He held her tighter, his voice fierce with determination. "We'll be ready. We'll protect our family. No matter what."

As they left the warehouse, the city's lights flickered in the distance, a beacon of hope in the darkness. Isis knew the battle was far from over, but she also knew they had taken the first step toward reclaiming their lives. With Jowan by her side, she was ready to face whatever came next.

Chapter 8: Choosing Sides

The tension in the cabin was thick as Jowan and Isis returned from their confrontation with Jamal. Kiana was asleep in the back room, blissfully unaware of the chaos that had unfolded. Isis sank onto the couch, her hands still trembling from the adrenaline. Jowan paced the room, his mind racing.

"We gotta be ready for whatever Jamal throws at us," Jowan said, his voice low and urgent. "He ain't gonna back down easy."

Isis nodded, feeling a knot of fear tighten in her stomach. "I know. But how do we stay ahead of him? We can't live like this forever."

Jowan stopped pacing and sat beside her, taking her hand. "We'll figure it out. We got Marcus and some other folks on our side. We just need to stay strong and stay together."

As if on cue, there was a knock at the door. Jowan grabbed his gun, signaling for Isis to stay back. He opened the door cautiously to reveal Marcus, his face grim.

"What's the news?" Jowan asked, stepping aside to let Marcus in.

Marcus glanced around, making sure no one was listening. "Jamal's been rallyin' his crew. He's pissed and lookin' for blood. We gotta be smart about this."

Isis felt a surge of panic. "What do we do, Marcus? We can't keep running."

Marcus nodded. "I know. We need to make a stand. Show him we ain't scared. But we gotta be careful. He's got connections, and he ain't afraid to use 'em."

Jowan clenched his jaw, his eyes filled with determination. "We need to hit him where it hurts. Cut off his support, make him realize he's alone in this."

Marcus agreed. "I got a plan. But it's risky. We need to take out his main supplier, the guy funding his operations. Without that, Jamal's got nothin.'"

Isis looked between them, feeling a mix of fear and hope. "What do you need us to do?"

Marcus laid out the plan, detailing their roles and the steps they needed to take. It was dangerous, but it was their best shot at taking Jamal down. They spent the next few hours preparing, gathering supplies and going over the plan.

As night fell, they set out, the city's streets a labyrinth of shadows and danger. They moved quickly, keeping to the back alleys and avoiding any attention. The tension was palpable, every sound making Isis's heart race.

They reached the supplier's hideout, a dilapidated warehouse on the outskirts of the city. Marcus led the way, his eyes scanning the area for any signs of trouble. They slipped inside, the darkness swallowing them whole.

Inside, the air was thick with the smell of smoke and sweat. Voices echoed through the halls, angry and tense. Marcus signaled for them to split up, and Isis felt her pulse quicken as she followed Jowan deeper into the labyrinth.

They found the supplier in a back room, surrounded by his goons. Marcus stepped forward, his voice cold and steady. "We need to talk."

The supplier looked up, his eyes narrowing. "Who the fuck are you?"

Marcus didn't flinch. "We're here to make a deal. You cut off Jamal, and we'll make it worth your while."

The supplier laughed, a harsh, grating sound. "You think you can just walk in here and make demands? You got some nerve."

Jowan stepped forward, his voice deadly calm. "We're not askin'. We're tellin'. You cut off Jamal, or we cut you off."

The room erupted into chaos. The supplier's goons lunged at them, fists flying. Jowan and Marcus fought back, their movements swift and precise. Isis watched in horror as the violence unfolded, her heart pounding in her chest.

She raised her gun, her hands shaking. "Stop! Everyone, stop!"

The room fell silent, all eyes turning to her. The supplier sneered, blood dripping from his nose. "You gonna shoot me, girl? Go ahead. Do it."

Isis's hands trembled, but she held her ground. "This ends now. You cut off Jamal, or we take you down. Your choice."

The supplier glared at her, but something in her eyes made him hesitate. He lowered his fists, a bitter smile twisting his lips. "Fine. You win. Jamal's cut off."

The tension in the room eased, but the danger was far from over. They left the warehouse, the city's lights flickering in the distance. Isis knew the battle was just beginning, but they had taken the first step toward reclaiming their lives.

As they drove back to the cabin, Jowan reached over and took her hand. "You did good, Isis. We couldn't have done it without you."

She squeezed his hand, feeling a surge of hope. "We're gonna get through this. Together."

The night was filled with plans and whispers, a constant reminder of the fight ahead. But for the first time in a long time, Isis felt a sense of peace. They had made a stand, and they were ready to face whatever came next.

The city's streets were unforgiving, but love was stronger. And with Jowan by her side, Isis was determined to protect what mattered most. The fight was far from over, but she was ready to win.

Chapter 9: The Ultimate Showdown

Isis woke up to the sound of sirens wailing in the distance, the familiar chaos of the city creeping back into her mind. She rubbed her swollen belly, feeling the baby move. The uncertainty of the baby's paternity still gnawed at her, but she pushed the thought aside. They had bigger problems to deal with.

She rolled out of bed, careful not to wake Kiana, and headed to the kitchen. Jowan was already there, his eyes bloodshot from lack of sleep. He handed her a cup of coffee, his expression tense.

"Marcus called," he said, his voice low. "Jamal's not backing down. He's coming for us tonight."

Isis felt a chill run down her spine. "What are we gonna do?"

Jowan's jaw tightened. "We're gonna be ready. Marcus is bringing some guys over. We're gonna set a trap. End this once and for all."

The hours dragged by as they prepared. Marcus arrived with his crew, their faces grim. They armed themselves, setting up positions around the cabin. Isis tried to keep her hands steady as she loaded her gun, the weight of the weapon feeling heavier than ever.

As night fell, the tension in the air was palpable. They waited in silence, the darkness outside pressing in on them. Every sound made Isis jump, her nerves stretched to the breaking point.

Then they heard it—the roar of engines, the screech of tires. Jamal's crew had arrived. Marcus signaled for everyone to take their positions, and Isis crouched behind the couch, her heart pounding.

The door burst open, and Jamal stormed in, his eyes wild with rage. "Where are you, Isis? Come out and face me!"

Jowan stepped forward, his gun raised. "It's over, Jamal. You're out of moves."

Jamal laughed, a harsh, bitter sound. "You think you can take me down? You're nothing, Jowan. Always have been, always will be."

Before Jowan could respond, one of Jamal's men lunged at him, and the room erupted into chaos. Gunfire echoed through the cabin, the smell of gunpowder filling the air. Isis ducked behind the couch, trying to keep her breathing steady.

She heard a scream and looked up to see Marcus grappling with one of Jamal's men. Blood spattered the walls as they fought, the violence raw and brutal. Isis felt a surge of fear for Jowan and Marcus, but she couldn't afford to lose her focus.

Jamal's eyes found hers, and he snarled, raising his gun. "You think you can take my place? You think you can replace me with my own brother?"

Isis stood, her hands steady as she aimed her gun at him. "It's over, Jamal. You're done."

Jamal's face twisted with fury, and he fired. The bullet grazed her arm, the pain sharp and immediate. But she didn't falter. She pulled the trigger, the shot echoing through the room.

Jamal staggered, blood blooming on his chest. He fell to his knees, his eyes wide with shock. "This ain't over," he whispered, his voice weak. "This ain't over."

Jowan rushed to her side, his hands shaking as he checked her wound. "Are you okay?"

Isis nodded, her breath coming in ragged gasps. "I'm fine. It's just a scratch."

Marcus limped over, his face bruised but determined. "We did it. It's over."

Isis looked around the room, the bodies of Jamal's men scattered on the floor. The sight was grim, but she felt a sense of relief wash over her. They had survived. They had won.

As they secured the cabin, Isis felt the weight of the past few months lift off her shoulders. The fight was over, but the scars would take time to heal. She leaned into Jowan, drawing strength from his presence.

"We're gonna be okay," she said softly. "We're gonna make it."

Jowan kissed her forehead, his voice filled with love and determination. "We will. Together."

The sirens grew louder, and soon the cabin was filled with flashing lights and the sound of officers barking orders. They were taken in for questioning, the night a blur of chaos and confusion. But through it all, Isis felt a sense of peace. They had faced the darkness and come out stronger.

In the weeks that followed, they began to rebuild their lives. The threat of Jamal was gone, and they could finally breathe. Isis focused on her family, preparing for the arrival of her baby. The question of the baby's paternity still lingered, but it no longer haunted her. She had Jowan, and that was enough.

As she watched Kiana play in the yard, the sun shining down on them, Isis felt a surge of hope. They had been through hell, but they had come out the other side. The city's streets were unforgiving, but they had found their way. And now, they were ready to face whatever the future held, together.

Chapter 10: Resolution and New Beginnings

Isis stood on the porch, the morning sun casting long shadows across the yard. The air was thick with the sounds of the city waking up, a cacophony of car horns, distant sirens, and the chatter of people going about their day. She took a deep breath, feeling the weight of the past months slowly lifting off her shoulders. The battle with Jamal was over, but the scars it left behind would take time to heal.

Inside, Jowan was making breakfast, the smell of bacon and eggs filling the small kitchen. Kiana sat at the table, her eyes bright with excitement. "Mommy, when's the baby coming?"

Isis smiled, rubbing her swollen belly. "Soon, baby. Real soon."

The sound of a car pulling up made her tense, but when she saw Marcus step out, she relaxed. He walked up the porch, his expression a mix of relief and exhaustion. "Morning, Isis. How you holding up?"

She nodded, feeling a surge of gratitude for Marcus's constant support. "Better. Just trying to take it one day at a time."

Marcus smiled, a weary but genuine smile. "That's all we can do. We took care of Jamal's crew. They won't be bothering you anymore."

Isis felt a wave of relief wash over her. "Thank you, Marcus. For everything."

He nodded, glancing toward the house. "How's Jowan holding up?"

"He's good. We're just trying to move on, you know? Build a new life."

As they talked, Jowan appeared in the doorway, wiping his hands on a towel. "Marcus, come on in. Breakfast is almost ready."

They gathered around the table, the atmosphere lighter than it had been in months. They ate in relative silence, the comfort of shared company a balm to their weary souls. As they finished, Marcus cleared his throat, looking serious.

"There's something we need to talk about," he said, his eyes meeting Isis's.

She felt a knot form in her stomach. "What is it?"

Marcus hesitated, then continued. "We need to figure out what's next. Jamal's gone, but his associates might still be out there. We need to be prepared."

Jowan nodded, his expression grim. "We can't let our guard down. We need to stay vigilant."

Isis felt a surge of determination. "We'll do whatever it takes to protect our family. We've come too far to let anything else tear us apart."

Marcus looked at her, admiration in his eyes. "You're strong, Isis. Stronger than you know. We'll get through this."

As the weeks passed, life slowly began to return to normal. Isis and Jowan focused on building a new life for their growing family. They moved to a new neighborhood, far from the shadows of their past, and started fresh. The scars of their ordeal remained, but they were healing, day by day.

One evening, as the sun set over their new home, Isis felt a sharp pain in her belly. She knew it was time. "Jowan, it's happening. The baby's coming."

Jowan sprang into action, grabbing the hospital bag and helping her to the car. The drive to the hospital was a blur of pain and anticipation, but Isis felt a sense of calm. She knew she wasn't alone. Jowan was by her side, and together they could face anything.

Hours later, they welcomed a beautiful baby boy into the world. As Isis held him in her arms, tears streaming down her face, she felt a profound sense of peace. This was their new beginning, a chance to build a life free from fear and violence.

Jowan leaned in, kissing her forehead. "We did it, Isis. We made it."

She smiled, looking up at him. "We sure did. And we're just getting started."

As they settled into their new life, the challenges of the past seemed like a distant memory. They were stronger, wiser, and more determined than ever to protect what they had built. The streets had tested them, but they had emerged victorious.

Isis stood on the porch one evening, watching Kiana play with her new baby brother. The future was bright, filled with hope and possibility. She had found love in the midst of chaos, and now she was ready to embrace the new chapter of their lives.

Jowan joined her, wrapping an arm around her shoulders. "You ready for this?"

Isis smiled, leaning into him. "With you by my side, I'm ready for anything."

The sun set over their new home, casting a golden glow over the city. Isis knew the journey ahead wouldn't be easy, but she was no longer afraid. She had Jowan, Kiana, and their new baby. They were a family, bound by love and resilience, and nothing could tear them apart.

As the night settled in, they stood together, looking out at the horizon. The streets had taught them to be strong, to fight for what mattered most. And now, they were ready to face whatever the future held, together.

Chapter 11: Healing Wounds

Isis sat on the porch, the early morning light casting a soft glow over the quiet neighborhood. The chaos of the past few months felt like a bad dream, but the scars were still fresh. She watched Kiana play with her new baby brother in the yard, the sight bringing a bittersweet smile to her face. They had been through hell, but they had made it out the other side.

Jowan walked up, a tired but determined look on his face. He handed Isis a cup of coffee, his touch warm and reassuring. "Morning, baby. How you holdin' up?"

Isis sighed, taking a sip of the steaming coffee. "Tryin' to keep it together, you know? It's been rough, but we got through it."

Jowan nodded, sitting beside her. "Yeah, we did. But we gotta stay strong. Jamal's associates ain't gonna disappear overnight."

The sound of a car pulling up made Isis tense. She glanced at Jowan, fear flickering in her eyes. He reached for his gun, always cautious. But when Marcus stepped out of the car, Isis felt a wave of relief wash over her.

"Morning, y'all," Marcus said, his voice tinged with exhaustion. "Got some news."

Jowan's eyes narrowed. "What's up?"

Marcus leaned against the porch railing, his face serious. "Jamal's crew is still out there, layin' low for now. We can't let our guard down. They might try somethin' again."

Isis felt the knot in her stomach tighten. "So what do we do?"

Marcus took a deep breath. "We need to keep our eyes and ears open. Stay connected with folks in the neighborhood. Make sure we're always one step ahead."

Jowan nodded. "We'll do whatever it takes to protect our family."

Isis looked at Marcus, gratitude and determination mixing in her eyes. "Thanks, Marcus. We couldn't have done this without you."

Marcus gave a weary smile. "We're all in this together."

As the days turned into weeks, life slowly began to find a new normal. They moved to a different part of the neighborhood, hoping to leave the shadows of their past behind. The community was still buzzing with gossip, but Isis learned to navigate the complexities of her situation. People talked, but she held her head high, knowing she had survived the worst.

One afternoon, as Isis was cleaning the house, she received a call from her mother. "Isis, baby, how are you holding up?"

Isis smiled, the sound of her mother's voice bringing comfort. "We're okay, Ma. Just trying to move on."

Her mother sighed. "I heard some folks talking. They don't know what you been through. Don't let their words get to you, okay?"

Isis nodded, her resolve strengthening. "I won't, Ma. We're stronger than that."

As she hung up the phone, Jowan walked in, carrying a bag of groceries. "Everything good?"

Isis nodded, taking the bag from him. "Yeah, just talkin' to Ma. She's worried about us."

Jowan wrapped his arms around her, his touch soothing. "We'll be alright. We got each other."

That evening, as the sun set over their new home, Jowan and Isis sat on the porch, watching Kiana and the baby. The future was uncertain, but they felt a sense of peace. They had fought for their family, and they had won.

But the battle scars were still there. Jowan's face was a constant reminder of the violence they had endured, the faint bruises still visible. Isis touched his cheek gently. "I'm sorry you got hurt, Jowan."

He kissed her hand, his eyes filled with love. "Ain't your fault. We did what we had to do. We protected our family."

Isis leaned into him, drawing strength from his presence. "I love you, Jowan."

He smiled, holding her close. "I love you too, Isis. More than anything."

As the stars began to twinkle above, Isis felt a sense of hope. They had faced their demons and come out stronger. The streets had tested them, but their love had prevailed. They were ready to face whatever came next, together.

Life slowly settled into a rhythm. They found joy in the little things—Kiana's laughter, the baby's first smile, the quiet moments they shared as a family. The threat of Jamal's associates still loomed, but they refused to live in fear. They had fought too hard to let anything tear them apart.

One night, as they lay in bed, Isis felt the baby kick. She smiled, placing Jowan's hand on her belly. "Feel that?"

Jowan's eyes lit up with wonder. "Yeah, I do. Our future."

Isis nodded, tears of happiness in her eyes. "Yeah. Our future."

The journey had been long and filled with pain, but they had made it. Isis, Jowan, and their family were ready to face whatever came next, knowing that they had the strength and love to overcome anything. The streets had taught them resilience, but their love had given them hope. And with that hope, they were ready to build the life they had always dreamed of.

Chapter 12: A New Threat

The neighborhood was quiet as the sun dipped below the horizon, casting long shadows that seemed to stretch endlessly. Isis stood in the kitchen, preparing dinner, but her mind was miles away. The past few months had been a whirlwind of change, but the tension never fully disappeared. She couldn't shake the feeling that something was brewing.

Jowan walked in, his face set in a grim expression. He tossed his keys on the counter and pulled Isis into a hug. "We need to talk."

Isis looked up at him, her heart racing. "What's wrong?"

Jowan sighed, running a hand over his face. "Jamal's old crew is back. Marcus got word they're plannin' somethin'. We need to be ready."

Isis felt a chill run down her spine. "What do they want?"

"Revenge," Jowan said bluntly. "They ain't happy about how things went down. They're lookin' to make a statement."

Isis's hands trembled as she turned off the stove. "What are we gonna do?"

Jowan's jaw tightened. "We're gonna protect our family. Marcus is bringing some guys over tonight. We're gonna figure out a plan."

The hours dragged by as they waited for Marcus and his crew. Isis tried to keep herself busy, but the fear gnawed at her. Kiana and the baby were asleep, blissfully unaware of the danger that loomed. Isis glanced at the clock, every tick echoing in her mind like a countdown.

Finally, there was a knock at the door. Jowan opened it to reveal Marcus and a few other men, their faces hard and determined. They filed into the living room, the air thick with tension.

Marcus spoke first. "We got intel that Jamal's crew is plannin' to hit one of our spots. We need to take them out before they make a move."

One of the men, a tall, muscular guy named Rico, nodded. "We gotta be smart about this. Hit 'em where it hurts, make sure they know we ain't playin'."

Jowan glanced at Isis, his eyes filled with concern. "You and the kids need to lay low. Stay here, don't answer the door for anyone."

Isis felt a surge of anxiety. "What if they come here?"

Marcus stepped forward, his voice steady. "We won't let that happen. We'll be on 'em before they can make a move."

As the men strategized, Isis felt a mix of fear and anger. She was tired of living in constant fear, of having her family threatened by the streets. She wanted to fight back, but she knew she had to protect her children first.

Hours later, the men left, their plan set. Jowan pulled Isis close, his voice low and urgent. "Promise me you'll stay inside, keep the doors locked."

Isis nodded, her heart heavy. "I promise. Just be careful."

Jowan kissed her forehead. "I will. I love you."

"I love you too," Isis whispered, watching him walk out the door, the weight of the world on his shoulders.

The night was long and restless. Isis kept vigil by the window, her eyes scanning the darkness for any sign of trouble. Every noise made her jump, her nerves stretched to the breaking point.

She prayed silently, hoping Jowan and the others would come back safe.

Suddenly, the sound of gunfire shattered the silence. Isis's heart leaped into her throat as she grabbed the phone, her hands shaking. She dialed Marcus's number, praying he would answer.

"Isis," Marcus's voice was strained, the sound of chaos in the background.

"What's happening?" Isis cried, her voice trembling.

"We're under fire," Marcus said, his breath heavy. "Jamal's crew ambushed us. We're holding them off, but it's bad."

Isis's mind raced. "What can I do?"

"Stay put," Marcus ordered. "We'll handle this. Just keep the kids safe."

The line went dead, leaving Isis in a deafening silence. She clutched the phone, her knuckles white, tears streaming down her face. She felt powerless, trapped in the house while the people she loved fought for their lives.

Minutes felt like hours as the sounds of the battle raged on. Isis prayed for Jowan, for Marcus, for all of them. She prayed they would make it through the night.

Finally, the gunfire ceased, replaced by an eerie silence. Isis's heart pounded as she waited, the suspense unbearable. Then, she heard the sound of footsteps on the porch. She grabbed a knife from the kitchen, her body tense.

The door creaked open, and Jowan stumbled in, covered in blood but alive. "It's over," he gasped, collapsing into her arms.

Isis held him tightly, her relief overwhelming. "Thank God. Are you okay?"

Jowan nodded, his breath ragged. "We got 'em. It's over."

Marcus and the others followed, their faces etched with exhaustion and pain. They had won, but the cost was high. Isis looked around at the men who had fought to protect her family, her gratitude immense.

As they patched up their wounds and shared the story of the battle, Isis felt a renewed sense of strength. They had faced the darkness and emerged victorious. The threat was over, but the scars would remain.

That night, as she lay beside Jowan, Isis felt a mix of relief and determination. They had survived another storm, but the fight wasn't over. They would continue to protect their family, to build a future free from fear.

Isis knew the road ahead would be tough, but she was ready. With Jowan by her side, she could face anything. They had proven their strength, their resilience. And together, they would overcome whatever challenges came their way.

Chapter 13: Standing Together

The aftermath of the battle left the neighborhood in a tense hush. The sun had barely risen when Isis stepped outside, the air thick with the remnants of gunfire and tension. The streets were empty, as if the whole block was holding its breath. She took a deep breath, trying to shake off the lingering fear from the night before.

Inside, Jowan was in the kitchen, nursing a bandaged arm. Marcus was with him, both of them looking weary but determined. Isis knew they couldn't let their guard down, not even for a moment.

"Morning, baby," Jowan said, his voice hoarse.

Isis kissed his cheek, feeling the roughness of his stubble. "Morning. How you holdin' up?"

Jowan shrugged. "Been better, but we're alive. That's what matters."

Marcus nodded, his face serious. "We sent a message last night, but we can't get comfortable. Jamal's associates might try somethin' again."

Isis clenched her fists. "We can't keep livin' like this, always lookin' over our shoulders. We need to end this, once and for all."

Jowan exchanged a glance with Marcus. "We need to rally the neighborhood. Make sure everyone's on the same page. If they come for us again, we need to be ready."

They spent the morning gathering their closest allies, people they could trust. Word spread quickly, and soon their living room was filled with familiar faces, all sharing the same look of grim determination. The room buzzed with whispered conversations, the air thick with the weight of their collective fear and resolve.

Marcus stood up, his voice cutting through the murmurs. "Listen up, y'all. Last night was a wake-up call. Jamal's crew ain't gonna back down easy. We need to show them we ain't scared."

A woman named Keisha, known for her sharp tongue and fierce loyalty, nodded. "We gotta protect our own. They come for one of us, they come for all of us."

Jowan stepped forward, his eyes scanning the room. "We need to be organized. Keep watch, share information. If you see somethin', say somethin'. We're stronger together."

Isis felt a surge of hope as she looked around the room. Despite the danger, there was a sense of unity, a determination to stand together against the threat. They spent hours planning, setting up patrols and communication lines. It was a community effort, and for the first time in a long time, Isis felt a glimmer of hope.

That night, as the sun dipped below the horizon, casting long shadows over the streets, Isis and Jowan sat on the porch, watching the neighborhood come alive with activity. People moved quietly, setting up watch points, checking in with each other. It was a show of strength, a message that they wouldn't be intimidated.

As the night wore on, the tension remained thick, but there was a sense of solidarity that hadn't been there before. Isis kept her eyes on the street, her hand resting on the gun in her lap. She was ready for whatever came next.

Around midnight, the sound of footsteps echoed down the street. Isis tensed, her grip tightening on the gun. Jowan and Marcus were beside her in an instant, their eyes sharp.

A group of figures emerged from the shadows, moving cautiously. Isis's heart pounded in her chest as she recognized them. It was Jamal's crew, looking for trouble.

Jowan stepped forward, his voice steady and strong. "This is our block. You want a fight, you got one. But we ain't backin' down."

One of the men sneered, stepping closer. "Y'all think you can scare us? We ain't goin' nowhere."

Before anyone could react, Keisha stepped out from behind a car, a bat in her hand. "You best believe we ready to die for ours. You?"

The tension snapped like a rubber band. The street erupted into chaos as the two groups clashed, fists flying and weapons swinging. Isis fired her gun, the sound deafening. She fought with everything she had, her fear turning into raw determination.

In the midst of the chaos, she saw Jowan grappling with one of the men, their struggle brutal and intense. Marcus was holding his own, his movements quick and precise. The fight was fierce, the air filled with the sounds of violence and defiance.

After what felt like an eternity, the fighting subsided. Jamal's crew retreated, beaten and bruised. The neighborhood stood victorious, but the cost was high. Isis looked around at her friends and neighbors, their faces bloodied but proud.

Jowan pulled her into a tight embrace, his breath heavy. "We did it, baby. We stood our ground."

Isis nodded, her heart pounding. "Yeah, we did. But we gotta stay strong. This ain't over."

As the sun began to rise, casting a new light over the battered streets, Isis felt a sense of hope. They had faced the darkness and stood together. The fight wasn't over, but they were ready. United, they could face whatever came next.

The neighborhood buzzed with a renewed sense of purpose. They had shown their strength, their resilience. And as long as they stood together, they could overcome anything. Isis looked at Jowan, their bond stronger than ever. They were ready to face the future, together.

Chapter 14: Legal Battles

Isis sat in the courtroom, the tension thick as the walls closed in around her. The low hum of whispered conversations buzzed in her ears, the anticipation building to a fever pitch. She glanced at Jowan, who was sitting beside her, his face a mask of calm determination. This was their day in court, a chance to finally put the past behind them.

The judge entered the room, and the murmurs died down. "All rise," the bailiff announced. Everyone stood as the judge took his seat, then sat back down, the wooden benches creaking under the weight of their collective anxiety.

The prosecutor, a stern-looking woman with sharp features, stood up. "Your Honor, we are here today to address the charges against Jamal Thompson and his associates for their involvement in various criminal activities, including assault, drug trafficking, and attempted murder."

Isis felt a shiver run down her spine. The reality of their situation hit hard. This wasn't just a fight for survival anymore; it was a battle for justice. She squeezed Jowan's hand, drawing strength from his steady presence.

The defense attorney, a slick-talking man with a greasy smile, stood up next. "Your Honor, my clients maintain their innocence and assert that they were merely defending themselves against unprovoked attacks."

A scoff escaped Isis's lips. The audacity of their lies was infuriating. She looked around the room, seeing familiar faces from the neighborhood, all there to support them. This wasn't just about her and Jowan anymore; it was about the entire community standing up against the violence and corruption that had plagued their lives.

As the trial progressed, witnesses were called to testify. Marcus took the stand, his voice steady and clear as he recounted the events of that fateful night. "We were defending our homes, our families. Jamal and his crew came looking for trouble, and we weren't about to let them tear our lives apart."

The prosecutor nodded, her eyes narrowing as she turned to the defense. "Mr. Thompson's actions were not in self-defense. They were premeditated and calculated, intended to instill fear and maintain control over the neighborhood."

The defense attorney smirked, leaning back in his chair. "And what about the violence perpetrated by your witnesses? Are they not also guilty of taking the law into their own hands?"

Isis's blood boiled. She wanted to scream, to make them see the truth. But she knew she had to stay calm, to trust in the process. The judge's gavel brought the room to order, and the questioning continued.

When it was Isis's turn to testify, she took a deep breath and walked to the stand. The weight of the moment settled on her shoulders as she faced the court. "I've lived in that neighborhood my whole life. We've dealt with gangs, drugs, violence. But we never asked for this. We just want to live in peace, to raise our children without fear."

The prosecutor's questions were sharp, designed to highlight the threats and intimidation they had faced. The defense's cross-examination was equally brutal, trying to paint her as a willing participant in the violence.

"Mrs. Johnson, isn't it true that you have a personal vendetta against Mr. Thompson due to your relationship with his brother?" the defense attorney asked, his voice dripping with insinuation.

Isis met his gaze, her voice unwavering. "My only vendetta is against the violence and terror that has torn our community apart. We stood up because we had no choice. We defended ourselves because we were under attack."

The courtroom buzzed with tension as she stepped down from the stand. Jowan gave her a reassuring nod, his eyes filled with pride. They were fighting for their future, and they wouldn't back down.

The judge called for a recess, and Isis stepped outside, the fresh air a welcome relief from the stifling atmosphere of the courtroom. She leaned against the wall, taking deep breaths to steady herself. Jowan joined her, wrapping an arm around her shoulders.

"You did great, Isis. We're almost there," he said softly.

She nodded, leaning into him. "I just want this to be over. I want to move on."

"We will," Jowan promised. "We'll get through this. Together."

As they returned to the courtroom, the final phase of the trial began. The closing arguments were passionate and intense, each side making their case with fervor. The judge's gavel brought the proceedings to an end, and the jury retired to deliberate.

The wait was agonizing. Hours felt like days as they sat in the courtroom, the tension palpable. Finally, the jury returned, and the room fell silent.

The foreman stood, clearing his throat. "We find the defendants guilty on all counts."

A wave of relief washed over Isis. They had done it. Justice had been served. She turned to Jowan, tears streaming down her face. They embraced, the weight of their struggle lifting.

As they left the courtroom, the sun was shining, a new day dawning. They had faced the darkness and come out victorious. The road ahead was still uncertain, but they knew they could face it together. They had fought for their future, and now they could begin to build it.

The streets were still tough, but they had found their strength. And with that strength, they would protect what they had fought so hard to achieve. The battle was over, but their journey was just beginning.

Chapter 15: Finding Peace

Isis sat on the front steps of their new home, the sun setting behind the buildings, casting long shadows across the street. The neighborhood was quieter here, a welcome change from the chaos they had left behind. She watched Kiana and the baby playing in the yard, their laughter a sweet sound after so many months of tension and fear.

Jowan came up behind her, wrapping his arms around her shoulders. "How you feelin', baby?"

Isis leaned back into him, sighing contentedly. "Better. Feels good to have some peace, finally."

Jowan nodded, his eyes scanning the street. "We've been through hell and back, but we made it. We're stronger now."

Isis looked up at him, gratitude and love filling her heart. "I don't know what I would've done without you, Jowan. You kept us safe."

Jowan kissed her forehead. "We kept each other safe. That's what family does."

As they sat there, the peace was interrupted by the sound of a car pulling up. Isis tensed, but relaxed when she saw Marcus step out. He walked up to them, a broad smile on his face. "Y'all lookin' good. How's the new place treatin' you?"

Isis smiled. "It's good. Feels like we can finally breathe."

Marcus nodded, sitting down beside them. "I'm glad to hear that. You deserve it."

They talked for a while, catching up and making plans for the future. Marcus had been a rock for them through everything, and Isis was grateful for his friendship and support. As the conversation wound down, Marcus stood up, giving Jowan a firm handshake. "You take care of her, man. She's a strong woman, but even the strongest need someone to lean on."

Jowan nodded. "You know I will, bro. Thanks for everything."

As Marcus drove away, Isis felt a sense of closure. The past was behind them, and they were ready to move forward. She turned to Jowan, a smile on her face. "We're gonna be okay, aren't we?"

Jowan pulled her close. "Yeah, baby. We are. We're gonna build a life we can be proud of."

The days turned into weeks, and life settled into a new rhythm. Isis focused on her job, finding joy in the little things. Jowan took on more responsibility at work, determined to provide for their family. They spent evenings together, talking and laughing, the weight of their past slowly lifting.

One afternoon, as Isis was walking home from work, she saw a familiar face. Keisha, one of their old neighbors, was standing on the corner, looking lost. Isis walked over, her heart pounding. "Keisha? What you doin' here?"

Keisha looked up, surprise and relief in her eyes. "Isis! I've been lookin' for you. Heard y'all moved."

Isis nodded, pulling her into a hug. "Yeah, we had to get outta there. Too much drama."

Keisha sighed. "I hear that. Things got real messy after y'all left. I had to get out too. Needed a fresh start."

Isis smiled. "Come by the house. We can catch up."

Keisha followed her home, and they spent the evening reminiscing and laughing, the weight of the past few months easing with each shared memory. It felt good to reconnect, to know they weren't alone in their struggles.

As the night drew to a close, Keisha stood up, a smile on her face. "Thanks, Isis. I needed this."

Isis nodded. "Me too. You're always welcome here."

After Keisha left, Isis sat on the porch, looking out at the quiet street. She felt a sense of peace, knowing they had built something strong, something lasting. She turned to Jowan, who was sitting beside her, watching the stars.

"We did it, Jowan. We made it through."

Jowan smiled, his eyes filled with pride and love. "Yeah, we did. And we're just getting started."

Isis leaned into him, feeling the warmth of his embrace. The future was still uncertain, but they were ready to face it together. They had fought for their peace, and now they were ready to build a life filled with love and hope.

As the night settled around them, Isis knew they had found something special. They had survived the darkness, and now they were ready to embrace the light. Together, they could face anything. The streets had taught them resilience, but their love had given them strength. And with that strength, they would build a future they could be proud of.

Don't miss out!

Visit the website below and you can sign up to receive emails whenever Rachael Reed publishes a new book. There's no charge and no obligation.

https://books2read.com/r/B-A-WXARB-JGCPD

BOOKS 2 READ

Connecting independent readers to independent writers.

Did you love *Once a Cheater*? Then you should read *Street Exodus* by Rachael Reed!

In the heart of Richmond, Virginia, the streets ain't no playground. It's a battleground where sex, brutality, and crime rule the night. Four fierce women—Mia, Lira, Brianna, and Monica—find themselves at a dangerous crossroads, trapped by the toxic men who claim to love them and the violent turf wars that threaten their lives. These streets got no mercy, and every choice comes with a deadly consequence.

Mia, a tough-as-nails hairdresser, dreams of nursing school, but her abusive, drug-dealing boyfriend Tyrone ain't lettin' her go without a fight. Lira's got the voice of an angel but is stuck singin' for her pimp boyfriend Reggie, who won't let her shine.

Brianna's a single mom working two jobs to keep her son safe from Marcus, a ruthless gang leader who drags her deeper into danger. And Monica? She's a street-smart hustler with plans for a legit business, but her drug lord boyfriend Jay's bloody turf war threatens to destroy everything she's built.

In a city where whispers become bullets, and betrayal lurks around every corner, these women must band together and fight back. Their journey is a gritty, raw, and heart-pounding escape from the streets that have claimed so many. Every step they take is a gamble, every breath a fight for survival. As they navigate the treacherous path to freedom, they uncover secrets, face deadly confrontations, and make unimaginable sacrifices.

But in the end, not everyone makes it out alive. "Street Exodus" is a dark, gripping tale of resilience, loyalty, and the relentless pursuit of a better life. It's a story where the stakes are life or death, and the only way out is through the fire.

Brace yourself for an unfiltered, adrenaline-fueled ride through the gritty underbelly of city life. This ain't just a story—it's a battle for survival.

Also by Rachael Reed

Codefendant
Once a Cheater
Once a Cheater
Passport Bro
What Happens in Prison
Preference
Sprinkle Sprinkle
Street Exodus
Street Exodus
Street Royalty